White House Dog

Adaptation by Jamie White
Based on a TV series teleplay written by Dietrich Smith
Based on the characters created by Susan Meddaugh

HOUGHTON MIFFLIN HARCOURT
Boston • New York • 2011

For information about permission to reproduce selections from this book, write to Permissions, Houghton Mifflin Harcourt Publishing Company, 215 Park Avenue South, New York, New York 10003.

Library of Congress Cataloging-in-Publication Data is on file.

Design by Rachel Newborn and Bill Smith Group

ISBN 978-0-547-21076-6 pb
ISBN 978-0-547-39359-9 hc

www.hmhbooks.com
www.marthathetalkingdog.com

Manufactured in China / LEO 10 9 8 7 6 5 4 3 2 1
4500253744

MARTHA FOR PRESIDENT

Greetings, dogs of America! Vote for me to be your president!

Why would I make a good leader? Well, for starters, I'm a talking dog! Ever since Helen fed me her alphabet soup, I've been able to speak. And speak and speak . . . No one's sure how or why, but the letters in the soup traveled up to my brain instead of down to my stomach.

Now—as long as I eat my daily bowl of alphabet soup—I can talk. To my family: Helen, Baby Jake, Mom, Dad, and our dog, Skits, who only speaks Dog. To Helen's best human friend, T.D. To anyone who'll listen.

Sometimes my family wishes I didn't talk *quite* so much. But who can resist a talking dog? Besides, my speaking comes in handy. One night, I called 911 to stop a burglar.

So just think what I can do for you! As president, I'll ban "No Dogs Allowed" signs. Every pooch will have his own fire hydrant.

And humans everywhere will say, "Ask not what your dog can do for you. Ask what you can do for your dog!"

And so, fellow dogs, it's time for a change. It's time for you—yes, *you!*—to vote—

What?

You're not a dog? You're a *human*? And I'm supposed to be introducing a story about me and the president? But I thought this book was about me *as* the president!

Er . . . in that case, you'd better turn the page to get to the real story.

WANTED: PRESIDENTIAL POOCH

Martha loved to talk. She could talk all day. She could talk all night. Martha had never met or seen anyone who could talk as much as she did.

Until, one evening, Martha saw her match.

She was watching TV with her family and T.D. A man in a suit was giving a speech. A long, *looooong* speech.

"America has lots to do in the months ahead," the man said. "But together—"

Martha changed the channel. *Click!* There he was again.

"—rise to meet these tests—" he said.

Click! And again!

"—so our country—"

Click! Click! Click!

"He's EVERYWHERE!" Martha shouted. She pawed the remote. "Is this thing broken?"

"Don't change the channel," said Dad. "This is exciting."

5

Martha rolled her eyes. "Some guy making a speech? Big woof."

"He's not just any guy," said Helen. "He's our new president. He's on every channel because this is his first press conference. Yesterday was his first day on the job."

"Oh." Then Martha asked, "What's a president?"

"The leader of our country," said T.D. "Every four years, a bunch of people run for president. They shout and argue about who would be best. That's called debating."

"I'd be great at debating," Martha said.

"I'm sure you would," T.D. agreed. "Anyway, all the grownups in the country vote for the person they think would be the best leader. The winner gets to be president and lead the nation."

"What's a nation?" Martha asked.

"Well," said T.D., "it's easier to explain if I draw it."

T.D. sketched a house. Then he drew Martha in front of it.

"Okay, so there's you, right? And this is our neighborhood," said T.D., adding more houses and some people. "Our neighborhood is a part of our town, Wagstaff City. And our town is one tiny part of our nation, the USA."

He drew Wagstaff City as a tiny dot on a map of the United States.

"There are lots of other nations, too," T.D. said. "Like Mexico and Canada."

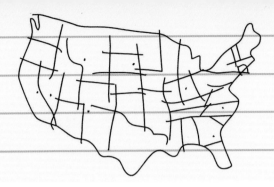

"Then what's a country?" asked Martha.

"*Country* and *nation* mean the same thing," said T.D.

"Then why don't people get rid of one of the words to free up space in the dictionary?" Martha asked. "If I were president, that's what I'd do."

"Hmm," said T.D.

"What? Can't a dog be president?" said Martha.

"I think only *people* can be president."

Martha sighed. "I don't know why dogs can't run for president," she said.

9

"I'd be a great leader. Free chewies for everyone! I hereby declare today as National Garbage Appreciation Day!"

"I'd vote for you," said T.D.

Yes, that's what this country needs, Martha thought. *A dog that everyone listens to!*

And then her wish came true.

Kind of.

"Last question, Mr. President," asked a reporter. "Is it true that you're looking for a dog to live in the White House?"

The president smiled. "Yes. One of my first tasks as president is to find a dog for my family."

Smart man, Martha thought. *No wonder he's president!*

The next day, the White House dog was all Helen, T.D., and Martha could talk about as they walked around town.

"I wonder if it has to be a real dog," said T.D.

"As opposed to a boy in a dog suit?" asked Helen, smiling.

T.D. shrugged. "Just asking."

"It wouldn't be fair to take the job away from a real dog," said Martha.

"You're right," T.D. said. "Hey, Martha! *You* should volunteer!"

Martha cocked her head. "Volunteer?"

"*Volunteer* means to do something helpful without getting paid," said Helen. "Like when you and I volunteered to help plant trees. You could volunteer to be the president's dog!"

"Me?" Martha said.

"Sure," said T.D. "I bet the president has never had a talking dog before."

Martha imagined life in the White House. *I'd get my own office! Hand-delivered hot dogs! Limo rides! I'd stick my head out every window!* She could already feel the wind at her ears.

"What would be my responsibilities?"
Martha asked. "Would I be the leader of the
dogs? Could I make bubble baths illegal?"

"No," said T.D. "It's more like fetching and
playing dead."

Poof! went Martha's dream of open
windows. *Instead of eating hot dogs in my office,*

I'd be doing my dead-dog routine, she thought.
Worse, I'd never see Helen.

"No," Martha said. "My home is here."

"Aww," said Helen, hugging her.

What's a dog without her family? Martha thought. This gave her an idea.

"Hey, I know a dog who'd be perfect for this job!" she said, running away.

"WHERE ARE YOU GOING?" Helen shouted.

But Martha was gone.

MARTHA INTERRUPTS

Psst . . . It's me, Martha. Can you believe I interrupted this story after only one chapter? But I *have* to tell you what happened next. (Hey, I gotta be me!)

There's a homeless dog I know who liked to hang in an alley.

"Hey, Smudge!" I called. "Are you here?"

Rattle, clunk. A small white dog with a dark smudge around one eye stepped out of a fallen trash can.

15

"Smudge," I said, "guess what? I think I found you a home!"

I told Smudge all about the president's search for a White House pooch.

Smudge was excited. He jumped and yipped . . . a lot!

Yip, yip, yip, yip, yip, yip, yip, yip, yip!

(Yes, Smudge is a yipper from way back.)

We went to my house to call the president.

Yip? Smudge asked as I dialed.

"Of course I know how to use a phone," I said. "How do you think I order pizza? Shhh— it's ringing!"

A lady answered.

"Is this the White House?" I asked her. "Great! I'd like to recommend someone to be the president's new dog."

Yap?

"What does *recommend* mean, Smudge? If you recommend someone, you say you think they'd be good at a job. I'm going to recommend you right now."

Smudge's tail wagged with joy.

"He's a dog named Smudge," I answered the White House lady. "Hold on. He's telling me something."

Yip, yip!

"He says he loves people," I repeated. "He only gets fleas in the summer. He can walk on his hind legs. And he's not a picky eater."

After I hung up, I walked Smudge to the doggy door. "The White House lady wouldn't tell me if you got the job or not.

But it was smart to tell her that you love people.
We'll have to wait and cross our paws."

Yip!

"My pleasure, Smudge."

Smudge must have done a lot of yipping
around town because there was a lot of yapping
at my doggy door that afternoon. I looked out
to see a line of dogs stretched around the house.
They all wanted to be the White House pet.

It was back to translation duties for me.

First came Rinty, the German shepherd.

"Rinty's a great watchdog," I told the White House lady. "The president would never have to worry about burglars. And—what's this?"

Rinty barked out a song. He couldn't carry a tune, but man, that dog had spirit!

"He can sing," I added. "Kind of. So he'd be terrific at parades."

Next came Bob, a mean-looking mountain of fur. He woofed what he wanted me to say.

"Bob has floppy ears," I reported to the White House lady. "He's big . . ."

WOOF!

"And what? Bob is *gentle!?*"

WOOF!

"Oh, I see," I said. "Bob is gentle as long as no one bothers him. Yes, everyone in our community just, um, appreciates him."

WOOF?

"*Community?*" I said to Bob. "A community is a group of people or animals who live in the same area. All of us in the neighborhood are a community."

WOOF?

"I don't have time to answer all these vocabulary questions, Bob! There are lots of dogs—" *Click*. The phone was dead. "Oh no. She hung up. I'll call her back."

I would have, too, but that's when Mom, Helen, and Baby Jake arrived.

"Martha!" Mom exclaimed. "What's going on? Every dog in town is outside!"

"Sorry," I said. "But since I made a phone call for one dog, it seemed only fair that I call for the others."

After Mom walked away, I made the rest of the calls. Then I made one last call. It was to order twelve pepp-eroni pizzas. The dogs were staying

to watch the evening news. We couldn't wait to hear which one of them the president picked!

I'd tell you who, but all this talk of pizza has made me *really* hungry. It's chow time. Talk to you later!

Yes. I said **12** pizzas!

TO THE
SHELTER!

The living room was packed with pooches.
After a while Helen squeezed in.

"The president spoke again today about . . .
what else? Getting a dog," said the reporter.

"Can we change the channel?" asked
Helen.

Grrrrrr, grumbled the dogs.

"Okay, okay," she said. "How long are we
supposed to watch this?"

"Shhh!" said Martha. "The president is
about to speak!"

"We would like to adopt a dog from an animal shelter," said the president.

The dogs groaned. Ears and tails fell as the dogs realized that none of them had been picked.

Animal shelter? Martha thought. *Why didn't he say so in the first place?*

Martha was a pound puppy herself before Helen adopted her. In fact, Martha knew the

Wagstaff City shelter very well. Kazuo, the
shelter manager, was her friend.

"Wagstaff City has a great animal shelter,"
Martha said.

At that, Smudge looked excited. He ran out
of the room. The others raced after him.

"WHERE ARE YOU GOING?" shouted
Martha.

An hour later, she learned the answer.

"You're still
watching TV?" Helen
called from the kitchen.
"You're becoming a newshound."
"Hound?" Martha sniffed,
offended. "I'm not just a hound! I
am a mutt of many breeds!"

"I just mean that you're watching a lot of news lately," Helen said.

"Shhh." Something on TV had caught Martha's attention.

"It's the strangest thing I've ever seen," said the reporter. "In the last hour, every dog in Wagstaff City has shown up at the animal shelter. Why? We're asking the manager now."

The reporter held a microphone up to Kazuo.

"I don't know what's going on!" exclaimed Kazuo. "They just burst in!"

Martha gasped. "*I* know!"

"Now you're *talking* to the TV?" said Helen, peeking in. "I think you've had enough news."

"I need to tell Kazuo what's going on!" Martha raced to the phone and dialed the shelter.

"Hello?" Kazuo answered.

"Hi, this is Martha! I know why all those dogs are there. On TV the president said he was getting his dog from a shelter," Martha explained. "All those dogs want to be picked."

"But the president isn't going to get a dog from *this* shelter," said Kazuo. "He'll go to a shelter near the White House."

"Is the White House far away?" Martha asked.

"It's in Washington, D.C. That's a gazillion miles *that* way!" said Kazuo, forgetting he was on the phone and pointing in the direction of the front door.

Martha heard Kazuo's muffled voice.
"Stop, dogs! You can't run all the way to
Washington! Watch out! Hey!"

Martha heard the phone drop and then the sound of many paws.

"Are you okay?" Martha asked.

After a minute, Kazuo answered. "I think so."

But things were not okay the next morning.

CAT CONSPIRACY

YIP-YIPPPPPP!

Martha and Smudge were watching the president cuddle something black and white and furry.

"The wait is over!" said the reporter on TV. "The president has finally adopted a dog, Chessie, from a Washington shelter. That's one lucky pooch!"

Smudge's hopes of having a family had crumbled like a stale doggy biscuit.

With drooping ears, he shuffled outside. Martha tried to cheer him up as they went to meet their friends at the fire hydrant.

"Take heart, Smudge. You don't have to live in the White House to be happy."

Smudge let out a weak yip.

"Come on," Martha said. "It's not that bad.
How about we all—"

"Martha!" Helen said, running up to their
doggy meeting place. She was very excited.

"You've got a phone call!"

"Huh?" said Martha, turning around.

"An important phone call. You'd better get it," Helen said.

Back inside their house, Mom held out the phone.

"Hello?"

"Is this Martha?" asked a familiar voice.

"Uh-huh."

"Hello, Martha. This is the president."

Martha froze. Was somebody playing a joke?

"Hello? Martha?" said the president. "*Helloooo?*"

"Psst, Martha," Helen whispered. "You're a talking dog. Say something!"

"Uh, yes!" Martha said. "I'm here! Are you really the *president?*"

"I am."

"Um . . ." Martha swallowed. "Can I help you?"

"Yes," he said. "One of my aides heard about your ability to talk. You're just what we need!"

"I am? Why?"

"I can't discuss that over the phone," said the president. "Can you come to the White House immediately?"

"Um, mum to the Hite Wouse? I mean . . . um . . ."

"Martha," the president said in a voice that meant business. "Your country needs you."

Me? For what? Martha wondered. Then it hit her. *Aha! The president must need my help in fighting a most horrible and unspeakable problem. A problem that can only be . . . cats!*

Martha imagined sneaky cats in dark alleys. *Secret cat meetings, she thought. Probably, federal agents secretly filmed them doing their dastardly deeds. It's a cat conspiracy to take over the nation!*

Duty called. Time to bust those cats!

"Mr. President," Martha said, "I'm on my way."

But before Martha left, she had to do one very important thing. Martha ran back to the fire hydrant to tell the gang.

"I'm going to the White House on an emergency mission!" she announced. "You know, a special job I was picked to do."

Yip!

"No, Smudge. I don't know what the mission is about yet. It's top secret. But I'm sure it has something to do with . . . *cats,*" Martha whispered.

Smudge listened. But the other dogs rolled their eyes.

"Did you not hear the part about a top-secret mission?" asked Martha. "You don't believe me? I swear it was the president!"

Smudge wagged his tail. The others looked away.

"My country needs me," Martha stated proudly. "I'll have an office! A candy dish of bacon bits! And when I get thirsty, my own toilet!"

Finally, the dogs raised their heads. They stared at something behind her.

"You're interested in toilets but not secret
missions?" Martha asked.

Beep! Beep!

Martha turned toward the sound of a car's
horn. A limo was waiting for her. The back
door opened.

"Come on," called Helen. "We have a plane
to catch!"

Martha happily leaped into the back seat.
As the limo drove away, she looked out the
rear window. That's when she saw Smudge
running after her!

Oh, Smudge, Martha thought. *I wish I could take you with me.*

But the limo sped off and Smudge was left in the dust.

BETWEEN DOGS

Martha stuck her head out every one of the limo's windows.

"This is just as I'd imagined it!" she shouted into the wind.

The limo drove to a private plane. On board, Martha sat by another window. She eagerly leaned toward it.

BONK! Her nose hit glass. "Ack!"

  "Sorry, Martha," said Helen. "These windows don't open."

When the plane landed in Washington,
another limo took Martha and her family to
the White House. But this was no ordinary
white house.

"Holy hamburgers!" said Martha, looking
around. "I've never seen a white house this big
and fancy!"

Inside, a man in a suit greeted them. He
walked them down a hall with old paintings
of men and women.

"Wow, the president sure has a large
family!" said Martha.

"Actually, these are portraits of past presidents and first ladies," said the guide.

"Oh." Martha looked around. "Where are the first dogs?"

"They don't paint portraits of the presidents' dogs," he said.

Martha gasped. "Why *not?*"

"Um . . . uh," the guide sputtered. "I'll make a note of it."

Martha smiled proudly. *I've made a difference already,* she thought.

The guide led them to the Oval Office. A lady stood behind the president's desk.

"Ooh!" said Helen. "This is where the president works."

But where is he? Martha wondered.

"Hello, Martha," the lady said. "Thank goodness you're here. I'm the special aide to the president."

"Hello, Ms. Special Aide," Martha said. "Here I am, ready to fight the cat conspiracy!"

The special aide looked puzzled. "What cat conspiracy?"

"Isn't that why the president called me?"

"No, it's not about cats. The problem's in here."

The special aide opened a side door to reveal another room. Inside, the president was on his knees next to a sad-eyed dog.

"Look, girl, a steak!" he said, pushing a silver dog dish toward his new pup.

Chessie lay on the floor, a sad furry lump.

"How about some chicken?" the president asked her hopefully. "Fish? Savory stew? Yum."

Nothing.

"I don't understand," Martha whispered.

"She's been like this all week," the special aide replied. "No one knows what's wrong. The president is so upset, he's no longer able to function."

"Huh?" Martha said.

"*Function* means to do a job," whispered Helen. "If he can't function, that means he can't do the job he was elected to do."

The special aide nodded. "Exactly. The president's plans for improving the nation stack up on his desk while he kneels here."

Martha covered her eyes. "I can't watch."

"The dog or the president?" Helen asked.

"The *steak!*" said Martha. "I can't watch delicious meat being ignored. Mmm."

The president looked up. "Martha, you're here!" he said, standing. "Thank you!"

Martha puffed out her chest. "Anything to serve my country."

"Martha, could you talk to Chessie and find out what's wrong?" asked the president.

"No problem, Mr. President," Martha said.

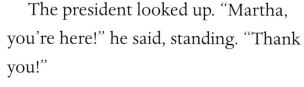

"But if I'm going to perform my function here, I'll need privacy."

At Martha's request the president ordered everyone out of the room.

This is different. The dog is giving commands to the humans. And I'm the dog. What fun!

Behind closed doors, Martha talked
with Chessie.

Soon Martha came out. She
whispered something into the aide's
ear, and the aide whispered
something into the
president's ear.

Whatever he heard made him snap his fingers.

His staff sprang into action. Instantly, the halls were full of workers with metal detectors and fancy tools. They searched and searched for something.

And finally . . . *BEEP-BEEP-BEEP!*

They found it.

"Call Martha!" a worker shouted. "Chessie's troubles are over!"

MARTHA SQUEAKS

Martha here. My turn! I want to tell this part of the story. This chapter tells how I really helped the president, and I don't want any important detail to be left out.

The special aide led me down a hall to a floor grate.

"Martha," she said. "They've found the item you wanted. Look!"

I gave the grate a good sniff. Yup. There it was, all right. Chessie's squeaky toy!

"Nice work," I said.

Chessie was thrilled to get her lost toy back. That squeak was music to her ears.

The president could work again, and Chessie was no longer a dog in the dumps. We played in the Oval Office all day. Serving my country was fun!

When it was time to go home, the special aide and my family came for me.

"Martha, wait!" the president said, stepping away from his desk. "Thank you for your help. It's great to have things functioning smoothly again."

"My pleasure," I said.

"*And*," he continued, "because of your ability to talk, your intelligence, and your sense of duty, I'd like to offer you a special appointment."

"An appointment?" I said. "Is that a reward? Like a presidential squeaky toy?"

"No. When you appoint someone to a job, you choose that person to do that job," the president explained.

"What kind of job?"

"To better serve the animals in this country, we need to know what they want. I'd like you to lead a task force to find out. You'd report back to me and my cabinet."

"Cabinet? Like that one?" I nodded to a wooden cupboard. Hmm. Reporting to furniture seemed silly. (Then again, I did talk to the TV.)

"No," said the president, shaking his head. "You're right. That *is* a cabinet. But the cabinet I'm talking about is different. The presidential cabinet is a group of people who advise me on how to take care of our people, forests, schools, and farms."

"Do they live in a cabinet?" I asked.

"No."

"Are they tiny enough to live in a cabinet?"

"No," said the president. "They're normal-size men and women."

"Then why do they call them a cabinet?" I asked.

"Beats me," said the president. "But they'd love to hear what the nation's animals are thinking. I'd like to appoint *you* to tell them."

"*Me?*"

"Yes. You'd be the first dog to lead a special task force. It's what you'd call a 'big woof.'"

"Wow!" said Helen. "Martha, this is a great honor."

"It's not everyone who gets called to serve the county like this," Mom said.

"I'll do it!" I said.

I began right away. With an aide to take notes, I traveled to every corner of the nation to speak with the common animal.

"Is there anything you want?" I asked a dog on the street.

Woof!

"More food," I translated to the aide.

"What do you want?" I asked an owl in the woods.

Hoot!

"More food," I repeated.

Squeak! Baa! Click! Moo! No matter what the sound, they all had the same answer: "*More food!*"

For the sake of my country, I even talked to a cat.

"Let me get this straight," I said. "You want a butler, a maid, a private room for the sandbox, and more furniture to claw? Plus, *what*? You want to make it illegal to have dogs?"

(I decided to ignore that last remark.)

Next, I returned to the White House to report my findings.

"The animals all agree on the food issue," I said. "The problem is these Washington fat cats. But cats are always a problem."

Chessie bounded over to play.

"Excuse me," I told them. "I have to handle something important. And, um, squeaky."

"Gimme that!" I said, chomping on Chessie's toy.

Squeak! Hee hee! That sound just *never* gets old!

"Ahem," the special aide interrupted. "Martha, the president and his cabinet are ready for you."

"Sorry, Ches. I have to go!"

I left her with her ears hanging low. Chessie depends on me as much as the president does.

MARTHA, PRESIDENT OF EVERYTHING

"In conclusion, Mr. President," Martha said, "the animals of this nation seem happy, but hungry. All except the cats. But then, cats are never happy. The end."

Martha sat at a table in the cabinet meeting room.

Next to her, the president patted her back. "Excellent report, Martha. You're a great advisor."

"Gee, thanks!" said Martha. "Um . . . one question."

"Yes?"

"What's an advisor?"

"An advisor is someone whose job it is to tell people all about a certain topic," said the president. "You've just advised us about what animals want and need. Now let's

hear what everyone else has to say. Secretary of State?"

A woman stood up.

"What's the secretary of state?" Martha asked.

"She's in charge of dealing with other countries," explained the president. "She helps make sure they all get along."

The secretary of state opened her mouth to speak.

"Has anyone ever thought about having a secretary of state for kids, too?" Martha asked. "Because what if the grownups of different countries get along, but the kids are fighting? I remember when Helen's cousin from Mexico visited. Oh, boy, was he a handful!"

The cabinet members exchanged confused looks.

Martha told them all about Helen's cousin and Mexico—and then beef tacos, chewies, Frisbees, fleas, and many other things . . .

When she stopped to catch her breath, the secretary of energy tried to get a word in. But when Martha heard his title, she couldn't help herself.

"Am I ever glad to meet *you!*" she said. "My dog friends and I have been discussing the energy crisis. We think we know why humans never have enough energy. You need more exercise! If people ran as much as dogs do, you'd have *lots* of energy. Instead of driving cars, try chasing them. Have you ever chased

a squirrel? Now, that's a good time. It's a shame you all don't have tails. Those are *really* great to chase . . ."

The president raised his finger to talk. It didn't work.

Running is just so much fun! Why, the other day, I ran after a delicious-smelling garbage truck for ten whole blocks, and . . .

The cabinet members began to fall asleep.

I've worn them out with all my good ideas,
Martha thought.

Before Martha knew it, the meeting was over.
The cabinet members hurried out the door.

"Is it over already?" Martha asked the
president.

"I'm afraid we only had three hours for that
meeting," he said.

"But I was just getting warmed up," Martha said.

The special aide appeared in the doorway. "Martha, I think Chessie needs you."

"Sorry, Mr. President," Martha said. "Gotta go."

"That's all right. We need to keep Chessie happy," he said. "Visit me when you're done. I want some people to meet you."

AMERICA, MEET MARTHA

When the president told Martha he wanted "some people" to meet her, she didn't think he meant the whole country!

In front of White House press cameras, the president introduced Martha to America. Of course, everyone in Wagstaff City gathered around TVs to watch the president praise his top dog.

"The happiness of animals is important to our nation," he said to reporters. "Luckily, we have someone who can speak for them. Thank you, Martha, for your service to this country."

The crowd cheered.

"Martha, do you have anything to say?" he asked.

But for once, Martha was speechless.

Martha's work in the White House had come to an end. She played one last game of tug of war with Chessie.

"Got it!" Martha said, squeaking Chessie's toy.

Chessie yipped with her nose in the air.

"Really? The president made a law that that's your toy?" Martha said, walking away. "In that case, there's nothing I can do except . . ."

Martha turned and pounced.

"Veto it!"

Chessie happily chased her, until Martha noticed visitors in the doorway.

"HELEN!" she cried.

"MARTHA!" said Helen.

Helen gave Martha a hug. Mom, Dad, and Baby Jake joined in.

"How did it go?" Dad asked.

"Great! I gave the president lots of useful ideas. Now I'm ready to go home."

Martha said her goodbyes. Chessie whined.

"I'll sure miss you, Chessie," said Martha. "Remember: Have fun and keep your toys away from the floor vents."

On the White House lawn, the special aide shook Martha's paw.

Just then, Martha heard scratching. She looked up. Chessie sadly pawed at an Oval Office window.

"Couldn't you stay to keep her company?" the special aide asked.

Martha shook her head. "Sorry. But if I don't have to serve my country anymore, I'd rather go home."

"Of course."

Poor Chessie, Martha thought. *She reminds me of another lonely dog I know.* Then Martha had her best idea yet.

"But," she told the special aide, "I think I know someone who could fill that function!"

That night, Martha snuggled with her
family in front of the TV. On the news, the
president's helicopter landed on the White
House lawn.

"Happy days in Washington this morning
as a new dog arrived at the White House,"
said the reporter. "His name is . . ."

A small white dog with a dark smudge
around one eye ran across the lawn and into
the president's arms.

"Smudge!" Martha said. "You're finally
home!"

MY PHONE BILL

You're still here? But you already read the happy ending! This story is over.

Good thing I always have more to talk about. Like what happened recently . . .

"What an adventure!" Mom said to Dad in the kitchen. "Our little Martha in the White House! It's history-making!"

Dad was paying bills. His eyes bulged as one unfolded all the way to the floor. "This long-distance phone bill is history-making!"

Uh-oh.

"Martha was just trying to help a few neighborhood dogs," said Helen.

"A *few?*" said Dad.

"If she hadn't called the White House, the president wouldn't have known about her."

"Well, I guess I'm glad it happened," said Dad.

Later that night, something else happened. Helen and I saw the secretary of energy giving a speech on the news. Behind a podium, he was jogging in place.

"To save energy, try running instead of driving," he said. "Running is just *so* much fun!"'

That's right about the time I began to fall asleep. Working for one's country takes a lot out of a pooch.

Good night, America!

Zzzzzzzzzzzzz End.

How many words do you remember from the story?

advisor: an expert whose job it is to inform others about a certain topic.

appoint: to officially choose a person to do a job.

cabinet: a group of people who advise the president on how to take care of people, forests, schools, businesses, and farms.

community: a group of people or animals with common interests who live in the same area.

debate: to discuss or argue about an issue.

function: to do a job.

mission: a special job one is given to do.

nation: a country, such as the United States, Canada, or Mexico.

neighborhood: a group of people or animals who live in the same area.

nominate: to officially recommend someone for a job.

president: the leader of the nation.

recommend: to say you think someone would be good at a job.

volunteer: to help out without getting paid.

A Quiz by Martha

To test your knowledge of the vocabulary words, Martha has created a quiz just for you. On a separate sheet of paper, vote for the definition you think is correct.

1. A *neighborhood* is
  a. something your neighbor wears on his or her head.
  b. a group of people or animals who live in the same area.
  c. the part of town where horses live.

2. An example of *community* is
  a. the group of dogs who live in Martha's neighborhood.
  b. the village of fleas who live on Bob's back.
  c. both of the above.

3. As leader of a special task force, Martha was on a *mission* to
  a. find out what animals want and need.
  b. become a competitive hot dog eater.
  c. appoint a personal belly-scratcher.

4. The *function* of a fire hydrant is
  a. to provide a source of water for firefighters.
  b. to serve as a colorful hangout for dogs to chat and do their business.
  c. both of the above.

5. A *president's cabinet* is
  a. a wooden cupboard.
  b. a group of tiny people who advise the president and live in a wooden cupboard.
  c. a group of normal-size people who advise the president on how to take care of the country (and do not live in a cupboard).

ANSWERS: 1.b 2.c 3.a 4.c 5.c

Martha Wants YOU to Vote!
A Quiz by Martha

Add up your correct answers. Then read what Martha says.

If you have . . .

5 correct answers, you are the *president*. Martha says, "You rule! Now try using your new vocabulary words when speaking with your friends and family."

3–4 correct answers, you are the *vice president*. "Way to go! Read and write every day and you'll soon be leader of the pack!"

0–2 correct answers, you are a *top-dog-in-training*. "No need to howl. Just study the list of words again. Keep practicing and you'll be a top dog!"